30119 024 309 199

D0245913

Fat Alphie in Love

Fat Alphie and Charlie the Wimp

Make friends with the greatest alley cats in town!

Be sure to read:

🐾 *The Disappearing Dinner* 🐾

... and lots, lots more!

Fat Alphie in Love

Noses are red
Noses are blue
Noses are black
And would you like
To come out with
On Saturday
night?

Margaret Ryan
illustrated by Jacqueline East

SCHOLASTIC

For Jane Harris with love – M.R.

LONDON BOROUGH OF SUTTON LIBRARY SERVICE	
02430919 ⁹	
Askews	Nov-2006
JF	

Scholastic Children's Books
Euston House, 24 Eversholt Street,
London, NW1 1DB, UK
A division of Scholastic Ltd
London ~ New York ~ Toronto ~ Sydney ~ Auckland
Mexico City ~ New Delhi ~ Hong Kong

First published by Scholastic Ltd, 2002

Text copyright © Margaret Ryan, 2002
Illustrations copyright © Jacqueline East, 2002

10 digit ISBN 0 439 99461 6
13 digit ISBN 978 0439 99461 3

All rights reserved

Printed in Singapore by Tien Wah Press

10 9 8 7

The rights of Margaret Ryan and Jacqueline East to be identified as the author and illustrator of this work respectively have been asserted by them in accordance with the Copyright, Designs and Patents Act, 1988.

This book is sold subject to the condition that it shall not, by way of trade or otherwise, be lent, resold, hired out, or otherwise circulated without the publisher's prior consent in any form of binding or cover other than that in which it is published and without a similar condition, including this condition, being imposed upon the subsequent purchaser.

Chapter One

All was not well at number three Wheelie
Bin Avenue. Fat Alphie's whiskers drooped,
his shoulders drooped and his tail trailed
along the ground.

"Why are you looking so miserable?"
asked his friend, Charlie the Wimp.

"I'm in love with Lovely Lola," sighed
Fat Alphie. "But whenever
I try to speak to
her she ignores
me. What can
I do to make her
notice me?"

Charlie the Wimp thought for a moment.

"Take her a present," he said. "Girls like presents."

"Good idea, Charlie," said Fat Alphie. "Let's go shopping."

They went to the "Purrfect Presents" shop
and bought a large box of Moggy Mint
Creams.

"Lovely Lola's bound to like these,
Charlie," said Fat Alphie. "They're
my favourite."

"Along with sugar mice, sherbert whiskers
and licorice tails," muttered
Charlie the
Wimp.

But Fat Alphie wasn't listening.

"We'll take these to Lovely Lola right now," he said.

They hurried along to number fourteen
Poshpaws Mews
and knocked
on the cat
flap.

The cat flap
opened and
Lovely Lola
slid outside.

"Hi Lola," said Fat Alphie. "I think
you're lovely. I've brought you a present."

Lovely Lola looked at the Moggy Mint
Creams.

"I never eat sweets," she said. "Don't you
know they make
you fat?"

And she
disappeared
back inside.

Fat Alphie's whiskers drooped, his
shoulders drooped and his
tail trailed along
the ground.

Even eating the Moggy Mint Creams all
the way back to Wheelie Bin Avenue didn't
cheer him up.

"Well, that didn't work, Charlie," he
sighed. "Now what am I going to do?"

They were just turning into number three
when Millie the Mouser darted past.

"Why are you looking so miserable, Fat
Alphie?" she asked.

"I'm in love with Lovely Lola," he sighed.
"But she ignores me. I've tried taking her
a present, but that didn't work. What can
I do to make her notice me?"

Millie the Mouser
thought for a moment.

"Sing her a song," she
said. "Girls like that."

"Good idea, Millie,"
said Fat Alphie. "I'll
sing her one I've made
up myself."

"Oh no," groaned Charlie the Wimp,
and put his paws over his ears. "Are you
sure that's a good
idea?"

But Fat Alphie
wasn't listening.
He hurried back
to number fourteen
Poshpaws Mews,
sat outside Lovely

Lola's window and began to sing…

"How much is that
    fat cat in the window
The one with the straggly tail
How much is that
    fat cat in the window…"

SPLOOOOSH!!! Lovely Lola emptied a bucketful of cold water over his head.

"Stop that racket this minute," she yelled, "and go away. Fat cat indeed!"

Fat Alphie's whiskers dripped, his shoulders dripped and his tail trailed in a puddle.

"I don't think she liked your song," said Charlie the Wimp.

Fat Alphie sighed and had to shake himself dry all the way back to Wheelie Bin Avenue. They were just turning into number three when One-eared Tom came round the corner.

"Why are you looking so miserable, Fat Alphie?" he asked.

"I'm in love with Lovely Lola," sighed Fat Alphie. "I took her a present, I sang her a song, but she still ignores me. What can I do to make her notice me?"

One-eared Tom thought for a moment.

"Write her a poem," he said. "Girls like that."

"Good idea," said Fat Alphie and hurried off to fetch some paper and a pen. Then he sat down and wrote Lovely Lola a poem.

"It doesn't rhyme," said Charlie the Wimp.

But Fat Alphie wasn't listening.

He hurried along to number fourteen
Poshpaws Mews and posted the
poem through the cat
flap.

Two minutes later it came back out
again. In bits.

"Told you it didn't rhyme," said Charlie the Wimp.

Fat Alphie sat on Lovely Lola's mat and drooped all over.

"Why are you looking so miserable, Fat Alphie?" asked Clever Claws, strolling past.

Fat Alphie gave a deep sigh.

"Cat got your tongue?" asked Clever Claws.

"He's in love with Lovely Lola," said
Charlie the Wimp. "But she ignores him."

"I sent her a present. I sang her a song.
I wrote her a poem. But she still ignores me,"
said Fat Alphie and sighed deeper than ever.

"That's because you're too fat," said
Clever Claws. "Lovely Lola only likes sleek
cats. You need to lose some weight."

"Lose some weight," cried Fat Alphie. "But I'm just cute and cuddly. I'm not really fat."

"Yes, you are," said all the other cats, gathering round. "You really are."

Then Fat Alphie looked so sad that Clever Claws said, "Look, come round to my place, and I'll lend you a book that might help."

❀ Chapter Two ❀

Later that night, after a dinner of tuna,
steak and chocolate cake, Fat Alphie picked
up the book Clever Claws had lent him.

"Look at the title, Charlie," he said.
"SLEEK IN A WEEK.
In seven days
we'll be slim."

"We!" squeaked Charlie the Wimp.
"You mean we, as
in you and me?
But I don't
need to lose
weight. If I get
any thinner
I'll disappear
completely!"

But Fat Alphie wasn't listening.

"The first chapter is all about exercising. We'll try some tree climbing first. That shouldn't be too difficult. I used to do that when I was a kitten."

The next day Fat Alphie and Charlie the Wimp went to the park.

"There's a little tree," said Charlie the Wimp. "We could climb that."

"That tree is a bush," said Fat Alphie. "What about that big oak over there?"

"But it's huge," said Charlie. "I can't even see the top. It probably goes all the way up to the moon. I don't want to climb all the way up to the moon!"

"Don't worry," said Fat Alphie. "It'll be easy. You go first."

Charlie closed his eyes and began to climb. "I'm getting dizzy. I'm sure I'll fall off," he moaned.

Fat Alphie took a deep breath and began to climb too. "Well, don't fall on top of me," he panted.

Finally they reached the top. Fat Alphie sat back, tired out. Charlie the Wimp clung on to him.

"I can't look down," he moaned. "How are we going to get back home?"

"Hmm, it WAS hard work climbing up…" said Fat Alphie thoughtfully.

Ten minutes later the fire brigade arrived.

"I don't know why cats climb trees," said the fireman who rescued them.

"Neither do I," moaned Charlie the Wimp.

Safely back at number three Wheelie Bin
Avenue, Fat Alphie opened the book again.

"I don't think tree climbing was a very
good idea," he said. "We'll try mouse
catching tomorrow."

SLEEK
IN A

"But I'm scared of
mice," cried Charlie
the Wimp.

Fat Alphie shook
his head. "YOU
are a very strange
cat," he said.

The next day they sat in wait by a mouse hole. Nothing happened.

"There's nobody home," said Charlie. "Let's go."

"Wait a minute," said Fat Alphie. "I'll check." He knocked on the side of the mouse hole. "Anybody in?" he asked.

"Who wants to know?" asked a large mouse, popping out suddenly and showing off some very sharp teeth.

"I do," said Fat Alphie.

"I don't," said Charlie the Wimp.

"We need to chase you for some exercise," explained Fat Alphie. "It says so in this book." And he showed the mouse SLEEK IN A WEEK.

The mouse looked thoughtful.

"Tell you what. Why don't we chase you for a change?"

And he put his claws to his lips and whistled up his gang.

"Oh no," yelped Charlie. "There's millions of them!"

The mice grinned and chased Fat Alphie and Charlie the Wimp all the way back to Wheelie Bin Avenue.

Chapter Three

Some time later, when Charlie had stopped shaking and Fat Alphie had got his breath back, they looked at the book again.

"Perhaps chasing a ball of wool would be easier," said Fat Alphie.

But it wasn't. Charlie the Wimp got
tangled up in it and it took
Fat Alphie all day to set
him free.

They rolled up the ball of wool and went
back to number three Wheelie Bin Avenue
to have a think.
"I think we
should give this
up," said
Charlie
the Wimp.

"And I think we should give the book one more try," said Fat Alphie. "I've got to be sleek for Lovely Lola."

"Okay," sighed Charlie the Wimp. "What about this chapter on diet?"

"I don't like the sound of it," said Fat Alphie, flicking through the pages. "Wait a minute, though," he said. "It says here that fish is good for cats, and I like fish."

"I like fish too," said Charlie. "It's my very favourite food in all the world. I like it for breakfast, dinner and tea. I like sardines, haddock, salmon, cod. Fat fish, thin fish, fish that come in a tin fish.

Big fish, little fish, somewhere in the middle fish. Wriggly fish, wiggly fish, slippery, slithery, squiggly fish. Oh, and prawn cocktail too."

"Okay, okay," said Fat Alphie. "Let's catch some fish."

They went down to the river with the ball of wool. They each cut a long piece and tied one end round their big toes. Then they lay down on the river bank to fish.

Fat Alphie closed his eyes. "This dieting is great," he said. "Why did I never try it before?" And he dropped off to sleep.

Soon Charlie felt a little tug on his toe. "I think I've got a fish," he cried.

But Fat Alphie was snoring too loudly to hear.

The fish tugged hard and began to pull
Charlie along the bank.

"I think I've got a big fish," he cried.

But Fat Alphie was too busy catnapping
to hear.

The big fish tugged harder and pulled
Charlie closer to the edge of the river.

"I think I've got a huge fish," he cried.

But Fat Alphie was too busy dreaming
about Lovely Lola to hear.

"It's pulling me into the water," cried
Charlie. "Help! Help!"

The huge fish tugged so hard it catapulted
Charlie right into the river.

He made a huge splash and soaked Fat
Alphie. That woke him up!

"Stop splashing me, Charlie," he yelled.
"Where are you?"

He looked up and saw Charlie sitting
on a large rock in the middle of the river.
The fishing line wool
was wrapped round
and round his
and round his
legs and he had
a huge fish in
his arms.

"You caught a fish, Charlie!" he cried.
"Well done. Throw it to me."

Fat Alphie caught the
fish just as Lovely Lola
strolled past.

"Oh how splendid, Fat Alphie," she said.
"I didn't know you were a keen fisherman.
You should have said. I just adore fish. It
helps to keep me looking lovely."

"I caught this specially for you, Lovely Lola," said Fat Alphie, and gave her the fish.

"Thank you very much, Fat Alphie," said Lovely Lola. "You don't mind if I call you Fat Alphie, do you? You're not really fat, just kind of cute and cuddly."

Fat Alphie smiled and smoothed his whiskers.

"But this is a huge fish," said Lovely Lola. "I couldn't possibly eat it all by myself. Would you and Charlie have dinner with me?"

"I'd LOVE to have dinner with you," said Fat Alphie, "just as soon as I've rescued Charlie. But I'm afraid he won't want to come. You see, Charlie doesn't really like fish."